PEARLS OF WISDOM

Growing in Grace; Maturing in the Lord

Geneva Green

PEARLS OF WISDOM
GROWING IN GRACE; MATURING IN THE LORD

iUniverse books may be ordered through booksellers or by contacting:

iUniverse
1663 Liberty Drive
Bloomington, IN 47403
www.iuniverse.com
1-800-Authors (1-800-288-4677)

ISBN: 978-1-5320-3828-0 (sc)
ISBN: 978-1-5320-3829-7 (e)

Print information available on the last page.

iUniverse rev. date: 12/24/2017

Pearls of Wisdom: PSALMS 29-2

Within these pages are some thoughts and comments I have on a number of subjects. Insights I've learned along the way and would like to share my point of view with its reader.

I want to start out by noting that I recognize and understand there are people who don't share my beliefs and philosophy of life; and I have no quarrels with their differences.

I've included the dates to note when I first put my thoughts on paper. But the dates may not be in chronological order and it may not flow in sequence. However, I hope who reads this will find some things that will connect and resonate with them and be helpful in some way.

08-26-2008

THE OVERCOMER:

Our victories in Christ has been established. They don't have to be fought again. When we faced our tests and overcame by our faith in God, it was a done deal. The same battles that were won does not have to be fought again. In these areas of spoils, we remain in authority. When we're emotionally drained, we can get alone with God and be refreshed by his Spirit. *Nothing is lost.*

07-30-2011

The Wonderful Blessings of Knowing God:

I believe that It'll be such a shame that we've squandered our time and not really gotten to know God when it comes our turn on life's stage on this Earth.

06-20-2016

Interpreting the Scriptures:

The quote: "You can make the Bible say what you want it to say." How this is sometimes done I believe, is by emphasizing the scripture verses that promote our agenda to make it agree with what we want it to say. This is why we need to know that the Bible is not for anyone's private interpretation. 2nd Peter 1-20.

And this is also the reason why each and everyone of us needs to develop their own personal relationship with God; studying the Bible to know what God is saying to them and learning how to apply it in our everyday lives. God wants each of us to establish that relationship with Him. And has provided the way to do that. St. John 3-16.

06-04-2014

Transitioning From This Life Into Eternity:

What we can and cannot take with us. There's a familiar saying that "You can't take it with you."

I believe we can take some things with us. We don't have to go into eternity empty-handed. When God gives us a ministry to fulfill here on Earth and this includes all types of ministries, be it secular or religious and we complete the ministry that is assigned to us, we take that crown and present it at Christ's feet when we bow before Him.

Only what God has called us to do will count. We cannot fulfill someone else's ministry and they cannot fulfill ours. Knowing what God has called us to do will make the difference. I don't believe we can take any material things with us.

07-18-2014

God's Answer to Prayers:

It's wise to wait for God to assure us that answers we've been praying for came from Him. When we pray for something, and an answer comes, wait for the Holy Spirit to witness that the answer came from God. Desire the answer, but not to the point that we're not willing to know where it came from. Let our love for God be superior to our desire for the answer. We need to be in relationship with God to know His leading.

05-29-2015

Life's Race: Hebrews 12 vs 1&2.

For every person born, I believe there's a race set before them. And no race is always the same. Based upon who we are our race is designed for no one else but us. Therefore, we cannot run someone else's race. It won't count for us; and knowing this should eliminate the need or desire for competition or envy.

When we stop looking at others and focus on the race that is set before us, we'll see our fellow man in a more positive light and have the energy and desire to accept the challenge that we're faced with.

May God grant each of us what we need to run our own race.

03-03-1998

Obeying our calling in life and using the strategy in the Book of Nehemiah to get the job done.

Nehemiah was sad because the city of Jerusalem was defaced. Its walls were broken down. When King Artaxerxes gave Nehemiah leave to go build the city back up, this is what he did.

1. He gave the king a set time of when he would return from doing the job. <u>He set a time.</u>
2. He kept it to himself what God had put in his heart to do at Jerusalem. <u>He kept it to himself.</u>
   2.a He went out at night to view the damages so that nobody could know what he was doing.

3. He had opposition to what he was called to do. They were Sanballat, Tobiah and Geshem. His opposition also despised Nehemiah for it. <u>Understand that you will have enemies and be despised.</u>

4. While the opposition scoffed, Nehemiah prayed and continued his work. <u>Keep on praying and keep on working until the job is finished. Don't be distracted by the opposition tactics.</u>

   4.a <u>Sanballat was angry and mocked the Jews when he heard that Nehemiah was re-building the wall.</u>

5. Nehemiah prayed to God and then set a watch against his enemies day and night. <u>After he prayed, he did something.</u> Pray and work.

6. Nehemiah told the people: Don't be afraid of your enemies because your Lord which is great and terrible will fight for you. He told them this after he heard that the opposition

was advancing toward them. Nehemiah got his people ready to fight. <u>Get ready to fight and don't be afraid.</u>

7. God's people worked with one hand and held their weapons in the other. Their swords were at their side. The men of God slept with their clothes on, just in case they had to go get up quick and do battle. They took their clothes off only to have them washed. <u>They stayed ready.</u>

    7.a God disarmed the enemy. <u>Always remember this: When God has called you to do a work for Him, He will take care of the opposition. Prepare yourself and leave the results to God.</u>

8. Nehemiah built the wall with no breach or opening left in it. When his enemies heard he had built the wall but left no opening, they tried to trick him to come down and meet with them somewhere. When they found out they could not get in to him,

they tried to trick him to come out to them. But Nehemiah wouldn't come out. He told them that he could not come down from the wall because he had too much work to do. <u>Don't be led away from what God has called you to do.</u>

9. His opposition group sent four more times asking him to come down, but he refused, giving them the same answer as he had the first time they asked. Then his opponents sent a fifth time. This time a letter accompanied. In the letter Sanballat tried to accuse Nehemiah falsely of rebellion. Another way to try and prevent the wall from being re-built. <u>Be alert to the ploys.</u>

10. Then Sanballat hired a prophet to prophesy falsely against Nehemiah in order to make him afraid. The prophet told Nehemiah to go to the temple and lock the doors so they won't kill you. They wanted everyone to be talking about how afraid Nehemiah

was of Sanballat. They wanted Nehemiah to look bad in the eyes of the people. They wanted to bring a reproach upon him. But Nehemiah didn't go. <u>Don't be afraid.</u>

11. Nehemiah finished the wall. So the wall was finished on the 25th day of the month. He finished building it in 52 days. <u>Finish up what God has called you to do.</u> *Nehemiah finished the wall.*

When all his enemies heard that the wall was finished and all the heathen saw what was done, they were much cast down in their own eyes because they perceived that the work had been wrought of his God. They realized they had made a mistake in trying to hinder him.

When God put something in your heart to do:

1. <u>Keep it to yourself.</u>
2. <u>Keep on working until the job is done.</u>

Trusting God on how to apply each of these strategies and to what situation.

1. Set a time.
2. Keep it to yourself.
3. Understand you will have opposition.
4. Keep on praying and keep on working until the job is finished. Don't get distracted.
5. After you pray, do something. Pray and work.
6. Get ready to fight and don't be afraid.
7. Stay ready. Always remember this: When God has called you to do a work for Him, He will take care of the opposition.
8. Don't be led away from what God has called you to do.
9. Be alert to the various ploys.
10. Don't be afraid.
11. Finish up what God has called you to do.

RELATIONSHIPS

02-02-2017

The Spirit of the Law verses the Letter of the Law. 2nd Corinthians 3-6 and St John 8-7.

Insight:

Jesus *demonstrated the Spirit of the Law* when dealing with a group of people who wanted to stone a woman to death who had been caught in adultery.

Coming to an understanding of why some things happen to people that cause them to behave, act or live a certain way or life-style. This includes people of all kinds, in all kinds of relationships; whether they're physically or emotionally abused, intimidated and every other kind of unwanted relationship.

For some people, the root cause is a lack of love and acceptance. Feelings that are at odds with each other, a dichotomy. Those opposing feelings clash. Galatians 5-17 gives us an explanation of this clash. And those feelings are aimed at causing people to feel guilt, shame alone and confused for being trapped.

Thinking they have no choice, people are forced into relationships they are opposed to and that tend to prey on them. But in cases where people still feel there is another choice, another option or avenue they can take, *There is One.* And this is it-St John 3-16. God's Love is to every human being. It's the great equalizer.

Don't come to expect something more in relationships that's not there. Don't expect more than people can give. Decide the kind of

relationship you can expect. Don't expect more that people can give. Decide the kind of relationship you can expect and proceed accordingly. Keep a balanced and proper perspective.

07-2016

God's Order and Design in the Universe:

We as human beings, we mess things up. And then things have to run its course for us to see the devastation of our doings before we return back to the way God ordered and designed things to work in the first place.

God's Laws are put in place for a reason. Spiritual, Moral, Physical, Cultural, Societal, and all other laws that governs the Universe. It's been said that History repeats itself. We get beside ourselves and think we're smarter than God.

10-02-2015

Gratitude:

I believe that we should live a life of gratitude instead of a life of grudge; wanting what others have. I think we waste our life doing that. I think we should be happy for them, but recognize the gifts we've been given and live our lives to the fullest with what we have. Our experiences and our convictions I believe, shapes us into the people we are. We don't all have the same experiences and that's what makes us unique. Living a life of grudge depletes us. It stirs up envy, hate, covetousness and other negative feelings that tend to weigh us down.

03-13-2012

Our Walk with God:

Amos 3-3. Can two walk together, except they be agreed? I'm not in competition with anyone else in my walk with God. God is all-inclusive, and I believe that competition takes the emphasis off of God and put it on the person; where it should not be.

Our walk is personal; and when we focus on fellow imperfect human beings as ourselves, whether to idolize them or find fault we somehow lose sight of the Perfect One; Christ our example. God has people in the Body of Christ I believe, that are serving Him in the capacity that he's called them to.

We're not all called to do the same work. When you know your calling, you can have peace with what you're doing though different maybe from someone else.

Printed in the United States
By Bookmasters